GORILLA GARAGE

by

Mark Shulman

illustrated by

Vincent Nguyen

two lions

two lions

Amazon Publishing
Attn: Amazon Children's Publishing, P.O. Box 400818, Las Vegas, NV
89140
www.amazon.com/amazonchildrenspublishing

Library of Congress Cataloging-in-Publication Data
Shulman, Mark, 1962-
    Gorilla Garage / by Mark Shulman ; illustrated by Vincent Nguyen.
        p. cm.
    Summary: A boy and his father see strange and unusual things when
their car breaks down and they are rescued by a gorilla.
    ISBN 9781477816639
    [1. Stories in rhyme. 2. Gorilla—Fiction. 3. Animals—Fiction.
4. Automobile repair shops—Fiction. 5. Fathers and sons—Fiction.]
I. Nguyen, Vincent, ill. II. Title.
    PZ8.3.S55977Go 2009   [E]—dc22
2008010736

The illustrations are rendered in pen and ink and colored in Photoshop.
Book and cover design by Vera Soki
Editor: Margery Cuyler

First edition

For the Rolanders—
John, Susie, Liza Rae, Lucy, and Charlie
—M. S.

For Anahid Hamparian and Margery Cuyler—
thanks for driving me bananas!
—V. N.

Papa and I took the car for a ride.
I asked to drive, but he laughed till he cried.

Going uphill the car shivered and sputtered.
"I can't believe it!" my poor father muttered.

Popping and screeching, the car began jerking.
Then the old motor just simply stopped working.

We sat and sat by the side of the road,
when a voice said: "Do you want to get towed?"

We were amazed at our wonderful luck,
until a gorilla stepped out of the truck.
Husky and hairy and seven feet tall,
he said, "I'm just coming back from a call.
See, it's my job to help monkeys who stall.
Mostly I don't stop for humans at all."

With giant arms and a casual look,
he hung our car on a huge metal hook.

"Hurry up! Hop in! And hang on!" he cried.
Papa looked small as they sat side by side.

Soon we arrived. Did I really read right?
"Gorilla Garage" blinked in pink neon light!
"Hey!" yelled our friend to another gorilla.
"Stalled on Route 90. That hill is a killer."

Two more gorillas appeared, big and gray,
picked up our car and just lugged it away.
Then we met three quite polite chimpanzees.
Bowing, they said, "Won't you come with us, please?
Just wait inside while your car's on the rack.
Sit. Read a magazine. Have a nice snack."

They set us down in a room painted green—
hot like a jungle, but comfy and clean,
with an electric banana machine.

Suddenly, in through the door burst an ape,
wearing a top hat, a tie, and a cape.
"Please," said the ape in a voice deep and strong.
"Where is my limousine? What has gone wrong?
You know that movie stars never wait long.
Please, sir, remember that I am a *Kong*!"

While the big ape was still making a scene,
I snuck away from my father unseen,
out to the place where they sell
gasoline.

That's where I found an orangutan crew,
pumping the gas as orangutans do ...
wiping a windshield with hands and feet, too.

Next came a pair of baboons in a van.
One hollered, "Fill 'er up fast, if you can!

Breakfast was bagels in north Baltimore.
And we'll be driving for twelve hours more.
Look at my bottom. . . . It really is sore!"

Back in the garage I heard noises inside.
That's when I tiptoed, I peeked, and I spied.
There was our car in the air for repair.
Maybe they'd catch me, but I didn't care.

Shining a flashlight and waving a wrench,
one gray gorilla was up on a bench.
Squirt! went the grease, and the motor was humming.
"Wait!" said a monkey. "The human is coming!"

Everyone stared, and I started to panic,
as I was grabbed by a hairy mechanic.
Gently he put me right down at the wheel
of our now-fully-fixed automobile.

"Drive," the gorilla said, and without fear,
I threw the car into fourth or fifth gear.
VROOM! went the engine, all ready for riding.
Papa ran out, screaming, "Where were you hiding?
Now you slide over," my dad said to me.
"We haven't time for this tomfoolery."

Then the gorilla just patted my head,
looked at my papa and here's what he said:
"Mister, the fixing was rather extensive.
Not only that, it was really expensive.
But if your son can remain at the wheel,
everything's free." And he winked.

"It's a deal?"

This couldn't be! Had I really heard right?
Would I be driving our car home tonight?

I looked at Papa, who just about cried.
All of us waited to watch him decide.

Then he slouched down, buckled up, and he sighed . . .
closed both his eyes and said, "Okay, let's ride."

Mark Shulman writes for children and adults. He's from Rochester and Buffalo, New York, where he worked at a gas station to make money while attending school. Now he lives with his family in New York City. Among his many books are *Mom and Dad Are Palindromes*, *A is for Zebra*, and *Not Another Tea Party*. Mark believes in giving service with a smile, even when you are covered in motor oil. And he actually knows someone who can make an emergency spark plug out of a paper clip and a potato.

Vincent Nguyen was born in Houston, Texas, and later moved to New York City, where he received a BFA from the School of Visual Arts. He has illustrated a number of picture books, including *Bandit* by Karen Rostoker-Gruber and *Little Britches and the Rattlers* by Eric A. Kimmel. He has also worked as an artist for animated feature films, such as *Robots, Ice Age 2*, and *Horton Hears a Who*. He lives in New York City.

22623563R00025

Made in the USA
Charleston, SC
28 September 2013